LENNY THE LOBSTER
— CAN'T STAY FOR DINNER —

by Finn Buckley *with* Michael Buckley
illustrated by Catherine Meurisse

For Sisi and Titi (Finn's cousins)
and Alison (Finn's mother)
—FB

For Elvira
—CM

Phaidon Press Inc.
65 Bleecker Street
New York, NY 10012

Phaidon Press Limited
Regent's Wharf
All Saints Street
London N1 9PA

phaidon.com

First published 2019
© 2019 Phaidon Press Limited
Text copyright © Finn and Michael Buckley
Illustrations copyright © Catherine Meurisse
Text set in Didot

ISBN 978 0 7148 7864 5
004–1218

Designed by Meagan Bennett

Printed in China

Lenny the Lobster was invited to a fancy
dinner party. He was delighted.

He put on his best hat, combed his moustache, and shined his claws. He looked dashing!

He had bought flowers for the hosts,

a yummy chocolate cake for dessert,

and bubble gum for the kids.

Every lobster knows it's nice to bring gifts to a party.

When Lenny got to the dinner party,
everyone was very excited to see him.

In fact, they seemed a little too excited . . .

They welcomed Lenny
with a gift of their own –
two tiny rubber band
bracelets for his claws.

"Why, thank you!" said Lenny,
"They match my hat beautifully."

8

Then everyone put on
a bib with a picture
of Lenny on the front.

"I had no idea I was the
guest of honor," Lenny said.

*HOLD ON! Are you getting a funny feeling about this party?
Do you think Lenny should stay for dinner? If you do, turn the
page. But if you think he should scoot out of there as fast as he
can, turn to page 22. Choose quickly! The guests look hungry!*

Lenny's hosts told him it was family tradition for
guests to take a dip in the hot tub before dinner.

"A hot tub sounds very relaxing," he thought.

So Lenny put on his swimming trunks,
looked down into the pot, and jumped . . .

. . . but little Imogen swept in and snatched him out of the air.
Before anyone could stop her, she whisked Lenny away.

"Young lady, what do you think you're doing?
This is very rude. You're ruining the party!"

Imogen wouldn't listen. She pedaled
all the way to the beach and do you
know what she did when she got there?

"You're free, Mr. Lobster. I've saved your life!" she cried.

"Good heavens, saved my life? You've only bent my moustache!" he shouted.

Lenny was beside himself. He knew
that if he didn't get back to the party,
he might miss dinner.

When he finally made it back, Lenny made sure that Imogen would not ruin his evening again.

WELCOME LENNY

He locked her out of the house.

"Now, let's get this party started! Woohoo!"

OH, NO! Lenny made the wrong decision by staying at the party. We can't let our story end this way! Go back to the beginning and when it's time to choose, make sure that Lenny does NOT stay for dinner!

Then, Lenny saw the butter. He saw a pot of boiling water. He heard growling bellies. Lenny HAD to get out of there!

He would not, could not, stay for dinner.
But his hosts were not yet ready to end the party.

He had been down this road before, and this time, he had come prepared. "You're messing with the wrong lobster!"

CAKE TO
THE FACE!

FLOWER POWER!

**BUBBLE GUM
CAVITY ATTACK!**

As Lenny fought his way through the
dinner party, a few things happened
that are hard to explain . . .

...but despite all of his clever tricks, there were just too many people to overcome. Lenny was trapped!

That is, until little Imogen came to his rescue! What's that she had in her hand? A Chinese food menu?

Well, it was a little awkward at first, but a good dumpling can fix just about anything.

"I can't believe you were going to cook me," chuckled Lenny. "That's hilarious!"

Everyone had a good laugh, until . . .

"Hey, they forgot to send us
the lobster chow mein!"

The end.